TORONTO BLUE JAYS
ALL-TIME GREATS

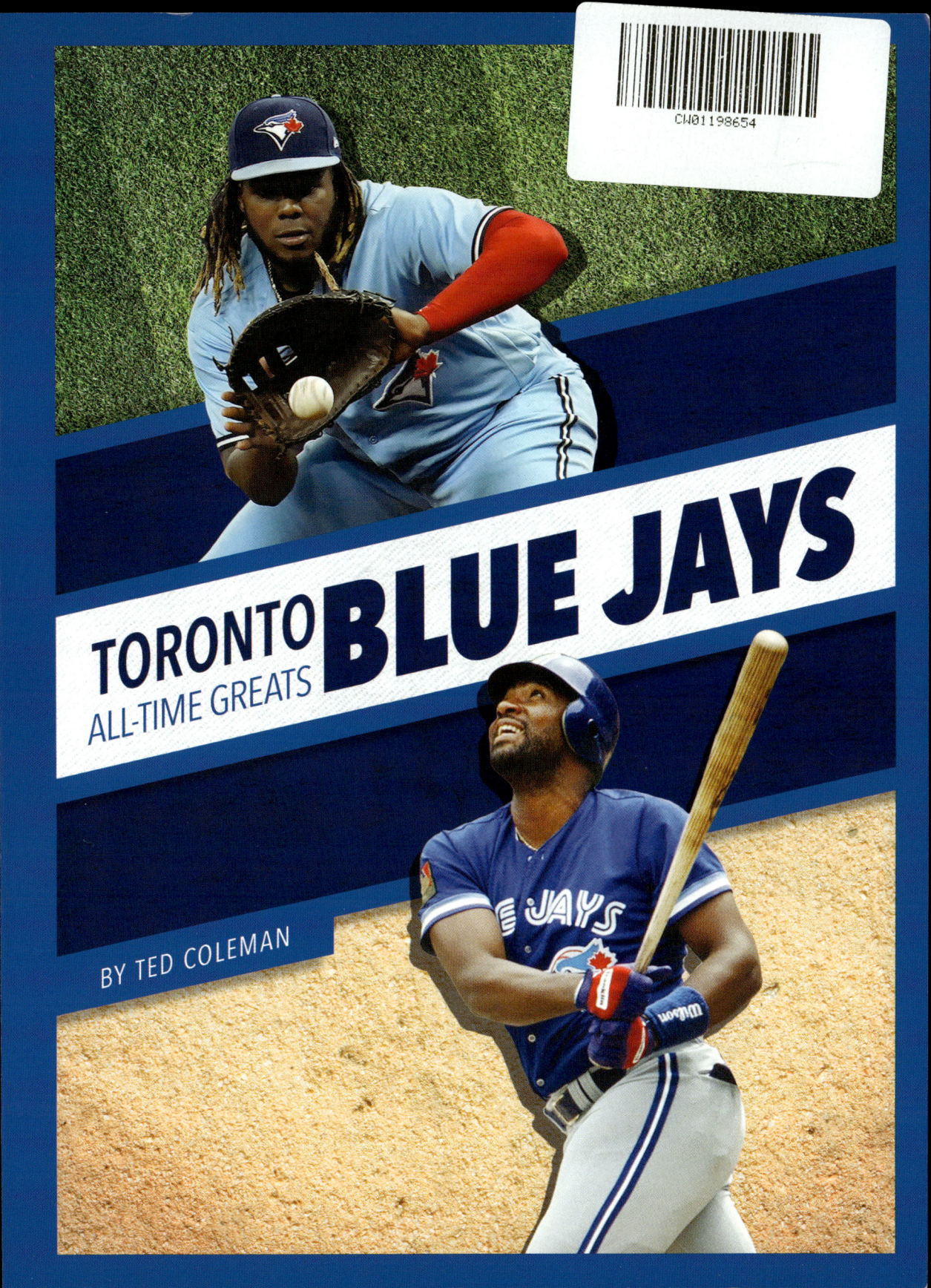

BY TED COLEMAN

Copyright © 2023 by Press Room Editions. All rights reserved. No part of this book may be used or reproduced in any manner whatsoever, including internet usage, without written permission from the copyright owner, except in the case of brief quotations embodied in critical articles and reviews.

Book design by Jake Slavik
Cover design by Jake Slavik

Photographs ©: Chris O'Meara/AP Images, cover (top), 1 (top); John Cordes/Icon Sportswire/AP Images, cover (bottom), 1 (bottom); Tony Dejak/AP Images, 4; Focus on Sport/Getty Images Sport/Getty Images, 6; Eric Risberg/AP Images, 8; Chris Gardner/AP Images, 10; John Cordes/Icon Sportswire, 13; Hans Deryk/AP Images, 15; Bernie Nunez/Icon Sportswire, 16; Mark Goldman/Icon Sportswire, 19; Gregory Fisher/Icon Sportswire, 21

Press Box Books, an imprint of Press Room Editions.

ISBN
978-1-63494-512-7 (library bound)
978-1-63494-538-7 (paperback)
978-1-63494-588-2 (epub)
978-1-63494-564-6 (hosted ebook)

Library of Congress Control Number: 2022901743

Distributed by North Star Editions, Inc.
2297 Waters Drive
Mendota Heights, MN 55120
www.northstareditions.com

Printed in the United States of America
082022

ABOUT THE AUTHOR

Ted Coleman is a freelance sportswriter and children's book author who lives in Louisville, Kentucky, with his trusty Affenpinscher, Chloe.

TABLE OF CONTENTS

CHAPTER 1
TAKING FLIGHT 5

CHAPTER 2
WORLD CHAMPS 11

CHAPTER 3
ACES AND SLUGGERS 17

TIMELINE 22
TEAM FACTS 23
MORE INFORMATION 23
GLOSSARY 24
INDEX 24

STIEB
37

CHAPTER 1
TAKING FLIGHT

The Toronto Blue Jays played their first season in 1977. However, they didn't win many games in their early years. Even so, Toronto fans knew their team always had a chance when **Dave Stieb** was on the mound. Stieb joined the Jays in 1979. The right-hander was a fiery competitor who challenged hitters. Only one pitcher in Major League Baseball (MLB) won more games in the 1980s than Stieb. And in 1990, Stieb threw Toronto's first no-hitter. During his 15 seasons with the Blue Jays, he made seven All-Star teams.

An increase in offense helped turn Toronto into a winner. A big part of that was the "Killer Bs" outfield of the 1980s. In left field stood **George Bell**. Bell had huge power at the plate. He also didn't strike out much. In 1987, that rare combo helped him win the first Most

Valuable Player (MVP) Award in Blue Jays history. Bell crushed 47 homers that year.

Lloyd Moseby held down center field. Moseby paired power at the plate with speed on the bases. His speed also helped him play great defense.

Jesse Barfield was the Killer B in right. Barfield struck out a lot. But when he connected, he could knock the ball a long way. Barfield also threw with a cannon for an arm. He won two Gold Glove Awards during his nine years in Toronto.

PAT GILLICK

Pat Gillick worked for the Jays from the very beginning. He began as an assistant general manager in 1977. He was promoted the next year. Gillick began assembling the team that would win a division title in 1985. Gillick's moves helped the team compete for World Series titles in the 1990s. He left Toronto in 1994 and eventually entered the Baseball Hall of Fame.

Tony Fernández became Toronto's starting shortstop in 1985. His great defense and hitting helped the Jays win their first division title that year. Fans loved Fernández. From 1986 to 1989, he won four Gold Gloves in a row.

By the mid-1980s, Stieb wasn't the Blue Jays' only star on the mound. **Jimmy Key** pitched at an All-Star level in 1985. He became a steady presence in the rotation just like Stieb. Key won more games for Toronto than any other left-hander.

In the infield, first baseman **Fred McGriff** supplied three 30-homer seasons from 1988 to 1990. In 1989, he led the American League (AL) with 36. All these players helped turn the Blue Jays into a winning team. But only a couple would be around when they won it all.

STAT SPOTLIGHT

CAREER HITS
BLUE JAYS TEAM RECORD
Tony Fernández: 1,583

HENTGEN
41

CHAPTER 2
WORLD CHAMPS

The Blue Jays played the 1992 season with Dave Stieb and Jimmy Key still in their rotation. Toronto also had youngster **Juan Guzmán**. Guzmán earned an All-Star spot that year. His pitches could be wild sometimes. But when he was on, Guzmán was one of the best strikeout pitchers in baseball.

Pat Hentgen started his Jays career in the bullpen. But in 1993, he entered the starting rotation. Hentgen pitched 10 years in Toronto. During that time, he made three All-Star teams. Then in 1996, he won the first Cy Young Award in team history.

After the 1990 season, Toronto traded Fred McGriff. That opened a spot at first base for **John Olerud**. Olerud nearly died in college from a brain injury. As a result, he always wore a helmet, even in the field. In 1993, he won a batting title and nearly won the MVP Award.

Throwing to Olerud from second base was **Roberto Alomar**. Alomar was starting a Hall of Fame career. He was exciting in the field and a great hitter. Alomar, Olerud, and Guzmán all played key roles in the Jays winning their first World Series in 1992.

OTHER HALL OF FAMERS

Three future Hall of Famers filled out the 1992 Blue Jays. Besides Roberto Alomar, there was pitcher **Jack Morris** and outfielder **Dave Winfield**. Winfield was 40 years old, and Morris was 37. But both players had great seasons and helped the Jays win a championship.

ALOMAR
12

13

In 1993, designated hitter **Paul Molitor** joined the roster. Molitor was nearing the end of a Hall of Fame career. But he played two of his best seasons in Toronto. Molitor batted .332 in 1993 and .341 in 1994.

Devon White didn't compare to Molitor at the plate. But White brought outstanding defense in center field. He won five Gold Gloves with Toronto.

Also manning the outfield was **Joe Carter**. The slugger made five All-Star teams with the Blue Jays. But he is best known for what he did in the 1993 World Series. In Game 6, Toronto trailed 6–5 in the bottom of the ninth. Carter stepped to the plate and hit a home run to win the game and the series. It was only the second World Series to end on a home run. It is widely considered the best moment in Jays history.

CARTER
29

DELGADO 25

CHAPTER 3
ACES AND SLUGGERS

Carlos Delgado won a World Series ring in 1993. But he only played two games that year. Delgado didn't really get a chance to show what he could do until much later. In 1996, he became a starter. Over the next nine seasons, he never hit fewer than 25 homers. And three times, he belted 40 or more.

STAT SPOTLIGHT

CAREER HOME RUNS
BLUE JAYS TEAM RECORD
Carlos Delgado: 336

The Blue Jays made a major splash after the 1996 season when they signed ace pitcher **Roger Clemens**. The legend had won three Cy Young Awards with the Boston Red Sox, but none since 1991. Clemens returned to his old form with the Blue Jays, winning the Cy Young in 1997 and 1998. But the fun didn't last for Blue Jays fans. Clemens asked for a trade before the 1999 season.

Fans soon got to cheer for an ace who stayed much longer. **Roy Halladay** joined the rotation in 1999. After a good start, he had a terrible year in 2000. But Halladay worked his way back. By 2002, he was an All-Star. Halladay's sinking fastball made him one of the most dominant pitchers in baseball. In 2003, he won Toronto's fourth Cy Young.

HALLADAY
32

The modern Jays have been loaded with home run hitters. **Vernon Wells** formed a powerful duo with Delgado. He had three seasons with at least 100 runs batted in (RBI). The center fielder also won three Gold Glove Awards.

José Bautista joined Wells in late 2008. Up to that point in his career, Bautista had been a utility player. But in 2010, he broke out with 54 home runs. That was a team record. He led the league again in 2011 with 43.

Designated hitter **Edwin Encarnación**

THE SONS

Vladimir Guerrero Jr.'s dad had a Hall of Fame career. But young Vlad wasn't the only Blue Jay with a big-league father. Shortstop Bo Bichette is the son of four-time All-Star Dante Bichette. And second baseman Cavan Biggio's dad, Craig, is in the Hall of Fame.

GUERRERO
27

arrived in Toronto in 2009. At the time, he wasn't a star. But before long, he was slugging right alongside Bautista and Wells. The trio all hit more than 200 homers in Toronto.

The next great Toronto slugger arrived in 2019. **Vladimir Guerrero Jr.** debuted at the age of 20. In 2021, he exploded to lead the league with 48 home runs. Fans loved watching how much fun he had playing the game. They hoped he would lead the franchise for years to come.

TIMELINE

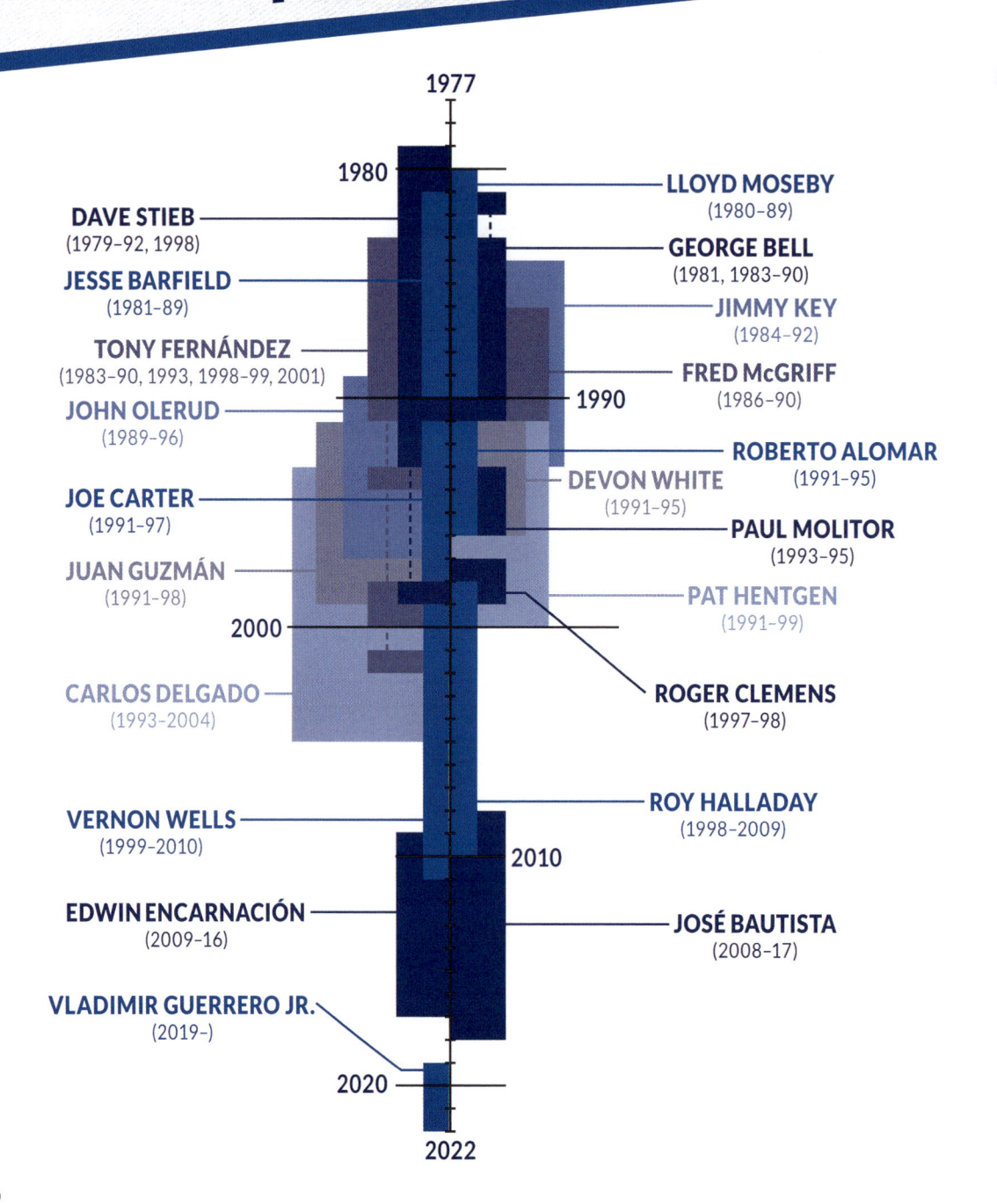

1977

1980

LLOYD MOSEBY
(1980-89)

DAVE STIEB
(1979-92, 1998)

GEORGE BELL
(1981, 1983-90)

JESSE BARFIELD
(1981-89)

JIMMY KEY
(1984-92)

TONY FERNÁNDEZ
(1983-90, 1993, 1998-99, 2001)

FRED McGRIFF
(1986-90)

1990

JOHN OLERUD
(1989-96)

ROBERTO ALOMAR
(1991-95)

DEVON WHITE
(1991-95)

JOE CARTER
(1991-97)

PAUL MOLITOR
(1993-95)

JUAN GUZMÁN
(1991-98)

PAT HENTGEN
(1991-99)

2000

CARLOS DELGADO
(1993-2004)

ROGER CLEMENS
(1997-98)

ROY HALLADAY
(1998-2009)

VERNON WELLS
(1999-2010)

2010

EDWIN ENCARNACIÓN
(2009-16)

JOSÉ BAUTISTA
(2008-17)

VLADIMIR GUERRERO JR.
(2019-)

2020

2022

22

TEAM FACTS

TORONTO BLUE JAYS

Founded: 1977

World Series titles: 2 (1992, 1993)*

Key managers:

    Bobby Cox (1982-85)

        355-292-1 (.549)

    Cito Gaston (1989-97, 2008-10)

        894-837 (.516), 2 World Series titles

MORE INFORMATION

To learn more about the Toronto Blue Jays, go to **pressboxbooks.com/AllAccess.**

These links are routinely monitored and updated to provide the most current information available.

*through 2021

GLOSSARY

ace
The best starting pitcher on a team.

bullpen
The area where relief pitchers warm up.

debut
To make a first appearance.

franchise
A sports organization.

no-hitter
A game in which a pitcher doesn't allow any hits.

runs batted in
A statistic that tracks the number of runs that score as the result of a batter's action.

utility player
A player who can play several different positions but is not good enough to be a starter.

INDEX

Alomar, Roberto, 12

Barfield, Jesse, 7
Bautista, José, 20–21
Bell, George, 6–7
Bichette, Bo, 20
Biggio, Cavan, 20

Carter, Joe, 14
Clemens, Roger, 18

Delgado, Carlos, 17, 20

Encarnación, Edwin, 20–21

Fernández, Tony, 8–9

Gillick, Pat, 7
Guerrero, Vladimir Jr., 20–21
Guzmán, Juan, 11–12

Halladay, Roy, 18
Hentgen, Pat, 11

Key, Jimmy, 9, 11

McGriff, Fred, 9, 12
Molitor, Paul, 14
Morris, Jack, 12
Moseby, Lloyd, 7

Olerud, John, 12

Stieb, Dave, 5, 9, 11

Wells, Vernon, 20–21
White, Devon, 14
Winfield, Dave, 12